FOX TAILS

The Great Bunk Bed Battle

Tina
Kügler

ACORN™
SCHOLASTIC INC.

For my dad, who never had to deal with this, because I was a perfect child—TK

All rights reserved. Published by Scholastic Inc., *Publishers since 1920*. SCHOLASTIC, ACORN, and associated logos are trademarks and/or registered trademarks of Scholastic Inc.

The publisher does not have any control over and does not assume any responsibility for author or third-party websites or their content.

No part of this publication may be reproduced, stored in a retrieval system, or transmitted in any form or by any means, electronic, mechanical, photocopying, recording, or otherwise, without written permission of the publisher. For information regarding permission, write to Scholastic Inc., Attention: Permissions Department, 557 Broadway, New York, NY 10012.

This book is a work of fiction. Names, characters, places, and incidents are either the product of the author's imagination or are used fictitiously, and any resemblance to actual persons, living or dead, business establishments, events, or locales is entirely coincidental.

Library of Congress Cataloging-in-Publication Data

Names: Kügler, Tina, author, illustrator. Title: The great bunk bed battle / by Tina Kügler. Description: First edition. | New York, NY : Acorn/Scholastic Inc., 2020. | Series: Fox tails ; 1 | Summary: It is time for bed but Franny and Fritz are arguing over which is the best bed: the upper bunk or the lower; they try switching but ultimately decide that the very best bed is Fred the dog's bed—so that is where they all curl up to sleep. Identifiers: LCCN 2019016958| ISBN 9781338561678 (pbk. : alk. paper) | ISBN 9781338561685 (library binding: alk. paper) Subjects: LCSH: Bedtime—Juvenile fiction. | Bunk beds—Juvenile fiction. | Brothers and sisters—Juvenile fiction. | Dogs—Juvenile fiction. | CYAC: Bedtime—Fiction. | Beds—Fiction. | Brothers and sisters—Fiction. | Dogs—Fiction. Classification: LCC PZ7.1.K844 Gr 2020 | DDC [E]—dc23 LC record available at https://lccn.loc.gov/2019016958

10 9 8 7 6 5 4 3 2 1   20 21 22 23 24

Printed in China   62

First edition, September 2020

Edited by Katie Carella

Book design by Sunny Lee and Sarah Dvojack

Ready for Bed

This is Fritz.

This is Franny.

This is Fred.

5

9

12

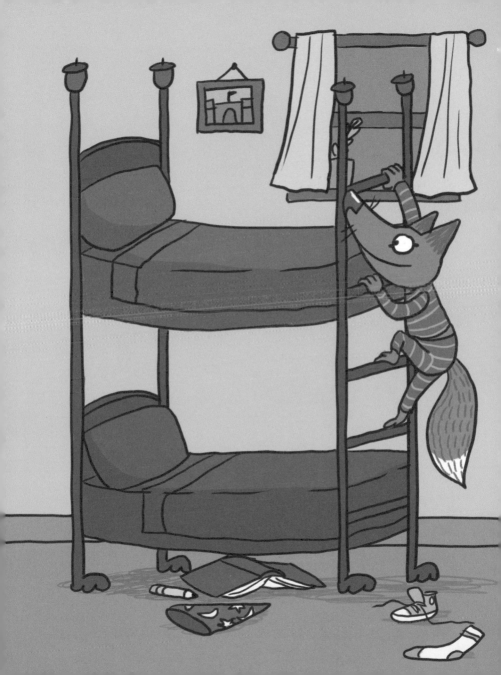

19

Come down here, Fred!
This is a cozy cave.

Look!
This is a high hilltop.

27

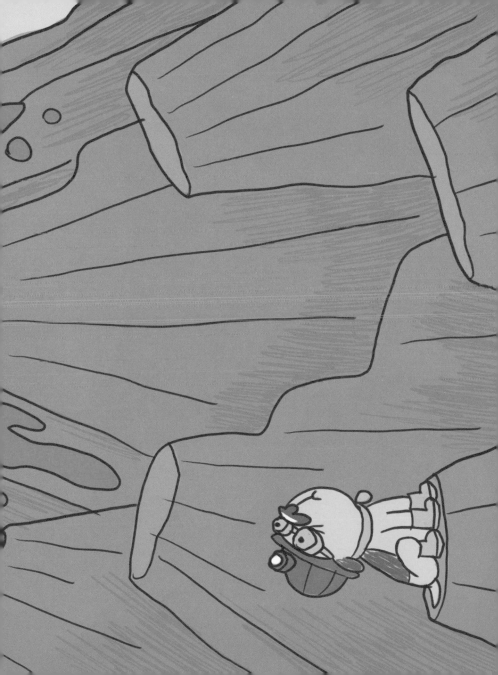

CLICK!

32

Let's Trade

The top bunk
is the very best bed.

No it is not.
The bottom bunk
is the very best bed.

Here, Franny.
You will love
the bottom bunk.

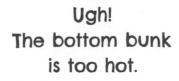

Ugh!
The bottom bunk
is too hot.

41

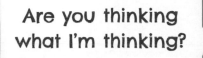

About the Author

Tina Kügler lives in Los Angeles with her husband and three sons. Her sons shared a bunk bed when they were younger, and they fought nonstop. That's actually what inspired this book

series! Even though her sons are older now, they are probably arguing while you are reading this.

Tina writes and illustrates books, and also draws cartoons for television. She wrote and illustrated the Snail and Worm beginning reader series and was awarded a Theodor Seuss Geisel Honor in 2018.

Oh, and she also has a cranky lizard named Jabba, a shy cat named Walter Kitty, and a cuddly cat named Freddie Purrcury.

YOU CAN DRAW FRITZ!

1. Draw two circles lightly with a pencil. (You will need to erase as you go along!)

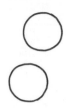

2. Connect the circles for Fritz's body and draw his nose.

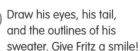

3. Draw his arms, legs, and ears. Fritz has long pointy ears!

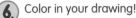

4. Draw his eyes, his tail, and the outlines of his sweater. Give Fritz a smile!

5. Add all the details. Don't forget his fang and whiskers!

6. Color in your drawing!

WHAT'S YOUR STORY?

Fritz and Franny's bunk bed takes them on adventures.
Imagine **you** share a bunk bed with Fritz or Franny.
Which bunk would you want and why?
What cool places would your bunk take you?
Write and draw your story!